Parents and Caregivers,

Stone Arch Readers are designed to provide enjoyable reading experiences, as well as opportunities to develop vocabulary, literacy skills, and comprehension. Here are a few ways to support your beginning reader:

- Talk with your child about the ideas addressed in the story.

- Discuss each illustration, mentioning the characters, where they are, and what they are doing.

- Read with expression, pointing to each word. You may want to read the whole story through and then revisit parts of the story to ensure that the meanings of words or phrases are understood.

- Talk about why the character did what he or she did and what your child would do in that situation.

- Help your child connect with characters and events in the story.

Remember, reading with your child should be fun, not forced. Each moment spent reading with your child is a priceless investment in his or her literacy life.

Gail Saunders-Smith, Ph.D.

STONE ARCH READERS

are published by Stone Arch Books, a Capstone Imprint
1710 Roe Crest Drive
North Mankato, Minnesota 56003
www.capstonepub.com

Library of Congress Cataloging-in-Publication Data
Klein, Adria F. (Adria Fay), 1947-
Circus Train and the clowns / by Adria Klein ; illustrated by Craig Cameron.
p. cm. -- (Stone Arch readers: Train time)
Summary: Many clowns in colorful costumes are riding on Circus Train.
ISBN 978-1-4342-4782-7 (library binding) -- ISBN 978-1-4342-6195-3 (pbk.)
1. Circus trains--Juvenile fiction. 2. Clowns--Juvenile fiction. 3. Colors--
Juvenile fiction. [1. Circus trains--Fiction. 2. Trains--Fiction. 3. Clowns--Fiction.
4. Color--Fiction.] I. Cameron, Craig, ill. II. Title.
PZ7.K678324Cis 2013
[E]--dc23   2012046900

Reading Consultants:
Gail Saunders-Smith, Ph.D.
Melinda Melton Crow, M.Ed.
Laurie K. Holland, Media Specialist
Designer: Russell Griesmer
Printed in China by Nordica.
0413/CA21300452
032013   007226NORDF13

Circus Train
and the
Clowns

written by
Adria F. Klein

illustrated by
Craig Cameron

STONE ARCH BOOKS
a capstone imprint

The Circus Train was back
in town.

Look at all the clowns!

There is one yellow clown.

He has a yellow flower.

There are two orange clowns.

They have orange balloons.

There are three green clowns.

They have green hats.

There are four red clowns.

They have red noses.

There are five blue clowns.

They have blue shoes.

Toot! Toot!

STORY WORDS

circus	flower	shoes
clowns	balloons	colors

Word Count: 69